Boom
Boom

Sarvinder Naberhaus

Illustrated by Margaret Chodos-Irvine

Beach Lane Books

New York London Toronto Sydney New Delhi

BEACH LANE BOOKS

An imprint of Simon & Schuster Children's Publishing Division

1230 Avenue of the Americas, New York, New York 10020

BEACH LANE BOOKS is a trademark of Simon & Schuster, Inc.

For information about special discounts for bulk purchases, please contact Simon & Schuster Special Sales at 1-866-506-1949 or business@simonandschuster.com.

The Simon & Schuster Speakers Bureau can bring authors to your live event. For more information or to book an event, contact the Simon & Schuster Speakers Bureau at 1-866-248-3049 or visit our website at www.simonspeakers.com.

Book design by Sonia Chaghatzbanian

The text for this book is set in Barcelona EF.

The illustrations for this book were created using a variety of printmaking techniques and nontraditional materials, including textured wallpaper, vinyl fabric, plastic lace, cut stencils, and pencil erasers.

Manufactured in China

0814 SCP

First Edition

10 9 8 7 6 5 4 3 2 1

Library of Congress Cataloging-in-Publication Data

Naberhaus, Sarvinder.

Boom boom / Sarvinder Naberhaus ; illustrated by Margaret Chodos-Irvine.

pages cm

Summary: An exploration of the four seasons, told through each season's distinct sounds.

ISBN 978-1-4424-3412-7 (hardcover) — ISBN 978-1-4424-3413-4 (ebook) (1. Stories in rhyme. 2. Seasons—Fiction.) I. Chodos-Irvine, Margaret, illustrator. II. Title.

PZ8.3.N16Bo 2014

(E)—dc23

2012043434

For Dr. Harpal and Harbhajan Bal,
with love
—S. N.

For Lena Mae
—M. C.-I.

drip

drip
drip

splash!

Bloom

crunch

crunch

fall

fall

bunch

bunch

Swirl

silent

silent

snow

snow